Dear Parents:

Congratulations! Your child is tak
the first steps on an exciting jour:
The destination? Independent reading!

STEP INTO READING® will help your child get there. The program offers five steps to reading success. Each step includes fun stories and colorful art or photographs. In addition to original fiction and books with favorite characters, there are Step into Reading Non-Fiction Readers, Phonics Readers and Boxed Sets, Sticker Readers, and Comic Readers—a complete literacy program with something to interest every child.

Learning to Read, Step by Step!

Ready to Read   Preschool–Kindergarten
• big type and easy words • rhyme and rhythm • picture clues
For children who know the alphabet and are eager to begin reading.

Reading with Help   Preschool–Grade 1
• basic vocabulary • short sentences • simple stories
For children who recognize familiar words and sound out new words with help.

Reading on Your Own   Grades 1–3
• engaging characters • easy-to-follow plots • popular topics
For children who are ready to read on their own.

Reading Paragraphs   Grades 2–3
• challenging vocabulary • short paragraphs • exciting stories
For newly independent readers who read simple sentences with confidence.

Ready for Chapters   Grades 2–4
• chapters • longer paragraphs • full-color art
For children who want to take the plunge into chapter books but still like colorful pictures.

STEP INTO READING® is designed to give every child a successful reading experience. The grade levels are only guides; children will progress through the steps at their own speed, developing confidence in their reading.

Remember, a lifetime love of reading starts with a single step!

*For Donna, who loves to
dance to the beat!* —D.L.

DreamWorks Trolls © 2017 DreamWorks Animation LLC. All Rights Reserved. Published in the
United States by Random House Children's Books, a division of Penguin Random House LLC,
1745 Broadway, New York, NY 10019, and in Canada by Penguin Random House Canada Limited,
Toronto, in conjunction with DreamWorks Animation LLC.

Step into Reading, Random House, and the Random House colophon are registered trademarks
of Penguin Random House LLC.

Visit us on the Web!
StepIntoReading.com
randomhousekids.com

Educators and librarians, for a variety of teaching tools, visit us at RHTeachersLibrarians.com

ISBN 978-1-5247-1842-8 (trade) — ISBN 978-1-5247-1843-5 (lib. bdg.)
ISBN 978-1-5247-1844-2 (ebook)

Printed in the United States of America
10 9 8 7 6 5 4 3 2

DREAMWORKS

TROLLS

DROP the BEAT!

by David Lewman

illustrated by Fabio Laguna
and Gabriella Matta

Random House 🏠 New York

DJ Suki plays music.
It thumps and pumps
from her Wooferbug!

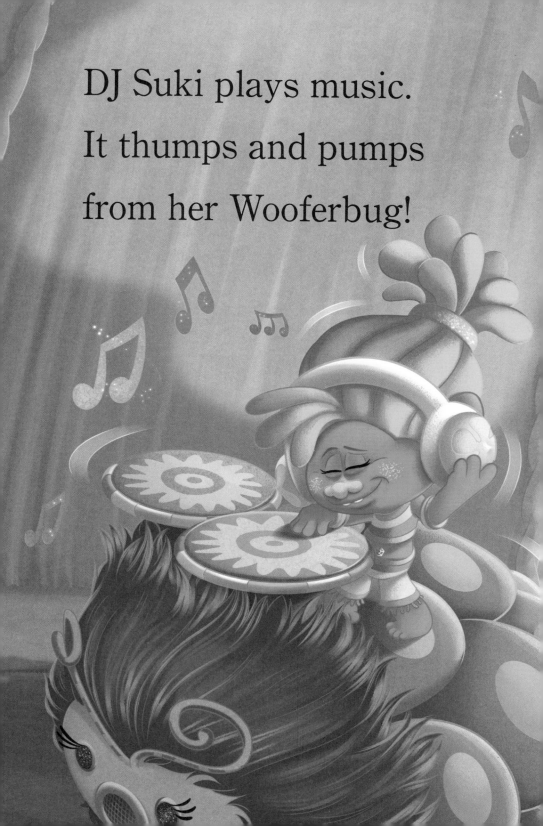

Biggie hears the music.
His pet, Mr. Dinkles,
bobs his head.
Biggie and Mr. Dinkles
love DJ Suki's music!

Biggie asks DJ Suki
what she is doing.
DJ Suki says she has
dropped the beat
on a new song!

That means she has
started the music,
but Biggie is confused.

Biggie thinks DJ Suki has *lost* her beat!

He and Mr. Dinkles
decide to find it
for her.

Biggie asks Cooper
if he has seen
DJ Suki's lost beat.

Cooper says no,
but he offers
to play his harmonica!

Biggie asks Fuzzbert
if he has seen
DJ Suki's lost beat.

Fuzzbert shakes his head.
Then he starts to hum
and whistle.
It sounds super
with Cooper's harmonica.

Biggie asks Guy Diamond
if he has seen
DJ Suki's lost beat.

Guy Diamond says no.

Then he starts to sing!

Biggie asks him

to come along.

Biggie asks
Satin and Chenille
if they have seen
DJ Suki's lost beat.

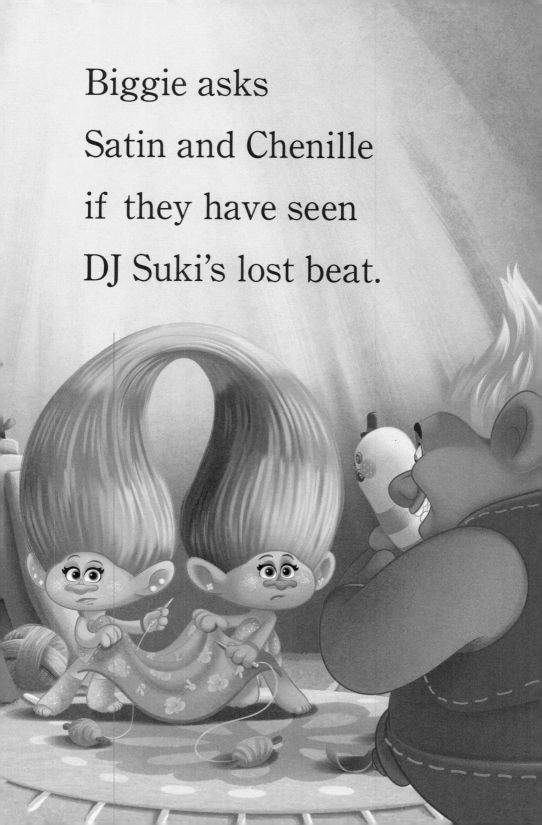

Satin and Chenille

say no.

But they can

sing harmony!

They will come along, too!

Biggie asks Poppy
if she has seen
DJ Suki's lost beat.

Poppy has not.
But she can play
her cowbell.
It sounds great!

DJ Suki loves
her friends' music.
She tells Biggie
that dropping the beat
just means starting
a new song!

She invites the Trolls
to add all their
wonderful sounds
to her music.

The Trolls play and sing
the new song together.
The music *rocks*!

More Trolls come
when they hear it.

The Trolls play,
dance, and sing
all night long!